FREEUSE OFFICE GAMES

A HOTWIFE SHARED

LACEY CROSS

TWISTED ROSE
· PUBLISHING ·

Book Cover by Steph Brothers

Paperback ISBN: 978-1-960162-24-3

About Freeuse Office Games

Some jobs come with very special benefits...

It's been far too long since I got to play at work, but when my boss proposes a special arrangement at the office, my husband Jon enthusiastically encourages me to accept. Suddenly, my typical workday involves a lot less paperwork and a lot more hands-on attention from four handsome lawyers.

But I wasn't expecting the senior partner to be so demanding, making me earn every moment of pleasure while testing my limits. Between impromptu meetings and surprise assignments, staying focused on actual work becomes increasingly challenging.

This week at the firm promises to be anything but boring.

CONTENTS

Chapter 1

I practically float through the office doors, my mind replaying yesterday's events on a loop. My body tingles at the memory of Mr. King using me and driving me crazy. I really hope no one expects me to do actual work today. I'm revved up and ready for more playtime.

The receptionist, Cindy, is on vacation, and the office is quieter than usual. Which is good, considering I'm the designated entertainment for four very sexy lawyers this week. The thought makes me squirm as I settle into my chair, smoothing down my pink button-down shirt.

Jon chose my outfit this morning, keeping in mind Mr. Jacobs' request yesterday that I wear my pink shirt. To go with it, my husband selected a white lace bra and panty set that he said would blow my boss's mind, along with a short black skirt and spiked high heels. Before I left, he kissed me and told me to

"Be a good slut for your bosses today." I'm not sure what I did in a past life to deserve Jon in this one, but it must have been something fabulous.

I'm logging into my computer programs when the instant messenger pings. My heart jumps into my throat when I see who it's from.

Mr. Jacobs:

Come to my office. Now.

Oh god–Mr. Jacobs is the senior partner at my law firm, and I love it when he gets demanding—especially knowing this might lead to something deliciously inappropriate that includes multiple HR violations. My spiked heels make me feel sexy and I put an extra swing into my hips as I make my way into his office. He's sitting behind his desk, devastatingly handsome in a charcoal suit. My mind flashes to previous times where his pristine suit was significantly rumpled when I left his office. It's been way too long since he's spanked me, and I think it's time to change that.

"Leave the door open. You won't be here long." His voice sends shivers down my spine. Dammit. I wanted the door closed.

He hands me a stack of papers. "These need to be completed within the hour. Miss one, and you'll find yourself back in here and bent over my desk."

My pussy clenches at his words. I scan the list on the top page, trying to focus despite the wetness growing between my legs. What the heck? I'm not in the mood to deal with my job today. He needs to rethink this plan.

"What if..." I pause, and give a sassy smile. "What if I want to be over your desk?"

"Let me be clear," he rumbles with authority, "your chance for an orgasm today depends entirely on your job performance. Understand?"

My pulse quickens. Oooh, stern Daddy Jacobs is out. Challenge accepted.

Lowering my lashes, I give him my best cutesy and contrite, "Yes, Mr. Jacobs," even though we both know I'm probably not going to do any of this paperwork. I'm sure he doesn't actually expect me to.

I rush back to my desk, but my mind refuses to cooperate. I'm too busy daydreaming about the past and remembering how much I loved being spanked by Mr. Jacobs–the heat that radiated from his palm, the lingering sting, the anticipation as I waited for the next strike. Also...each time I finish one task, the pile seems to multiply. I swear it's breeding.

I'm not even halfway through the pile when the hour is up. My stomach flutters with excitement as I wait for his summons.

When my instant messenger flashes, I expect him to ask me about the forms, but he doesn't.

Mr. Jacobs:

> Please set up the conference room and get coffee ready for the attendees.

Ugh. This is bullshit. My mind races as I do as I'm told. Where's my spanking for not finishing the forms? I'm the freeuse office slut. I was supposed to have four cocks inside me by now. After Mr. King fucked me all over the office yesterday and made me suck him off under his desk, I expected more today. I think the bastard is teasing me and making me wait for it.

My hands shake as I fill the coffee carafe and arrange the cups. I'm so turned on, I can barely think straight. As I'm finishing up, Mr. Jacobs comes in with a stack of papers and empty manila folders.

He closes the door behind him. "Miranda, you're crawling at a snail's pace today. You should be done by now."

I open my mouth to tell him that maybe if he had spanked me, I would have picked up the pace, but I quickly close it again. Yeah, probably not. I would have just wanted more.

I raise an eyebrow at him while he separates the papers into three piles and sets the empty folders next to them on the table.

"Each folder needs one of each form before the meeting starts. You have 10 minutes."

There wasn't a meeting on the calendar, and organizing folders this way definitely isn't how things are done around here. This is a set up if I ever saw one–and I'm okay with that.

He doesn't move away from the table and I have to crowd close to him to reach the forms. Daddy Jacobs is being a bit of a jerk, and with how wet my panties are, my slutty pussy loves it.

I quickly start filling the folders, but him watching over me is making me feel clumsy and I keep accidentally grabbing multiple sheets from the same pile. I'm about to snap at him and ask him if he doesn't have something better to do when he suddenly moves in behind me and unzips my skirt. Ohhh, hello.

My skirt pools at my feet and he rubs his hands over my panties. My pink button-down shirt had been tucked in, but now the ends trail down my stomach and ass. From where he's standing, I bet my legs look amazing in these heels.

When he rubs my pussy, I purposely jut my ass out towards him and his attention makes me inadvertently slow my hand movements.

"How long has it been since I fucked you?" he growls as he continues to run his fingers over the fabric covering my pussy.

"Two years," I breathe out softly. Most of our previous fun times at the office started with a punishment spanking that lead to sex. What he's doing now leaves me uncertain what to expect.

His hand lands on my ass in a sharp spank, and I gasp. Yeah, never mind, there it is.

"That's for being such a tease the last two years when you knew I couldn't fuck you."

Ooooh, god. What the hell? It's not my fault he couldn't fuck me. I'm not the one who hired Bonny, which turned out to be the demise of our office fuckfest. Since he's the senior partner, he would have had a lot of sway in their choice for office manager. Maybe HE should have thought of that when making the final decision. I moan when he spanks me again.

"Keep working," he says gruffly.

Fuck, okay. Must concentrate... Mr. Jacobs' spanks fall in a hypnotic rhythm, making it impossible to think straight. Each one sends jolts of delight through my body. I'm torn between the need to complete the folders and the overwhelming desire to close my eyes and bliss out. I'll just get them done quickly. My hands move on autopilot, shoving papers together.

"Time's running out," he warns as he delivers another painful spank.

When he pulls my panties down to my knees, I bite back a groan and grip the edge of the table. He slides a finger into my pussy and fucks me with it as pleasure swirls in my core. Um, how long have we been in here? Are people about to walk in?

He stops finger fucking me and I hear the sound of his zipper as the teeth slowly part. Every nerve ending sparks alive as the tip of his cock gently probes my pussy. Mmm, now this is more like it.

He grasps my hips firmly, his fingers digging into my flesh. I welcome the slight pain when he slowly sinks into me. Holy fuck, I forgot how much I love his cock after having gone so long without it.

He pauses once he bottoms out and I realize my hands have gone still. Oops, shit. I quickly start stuffing files again as delight ripples through me.

Mr. Jacobs pins my hips against the table with every slow thrust. It's almost impossible to concentrate. Although I'm hindered by my panties, I spread my legs as wide as I can to encourage him to fuck me harder, but he doesn't. Each drag of his cock along the sensitive nerve endings inside me makes my head spin and it doesn't take long for me to feel like I'm losing my mind from pleasure.

"The conference starts any minute now and you're only halfway done. I'm not rewarding your poor work ethic with an orgasm," he taunts me as he slaps my ass.

Ugh. What a jerk. I try to shuffle the pages again. Wait, where was I?

When he moves his hand around to my front and fingers my clit, I roll my hips and let out a small involuntary whimper. Oh fuck. My hands tremble as I haphazardly shove forms into the last few folders. I'm not even paying attention anymore to what I'm putting into each one.

When he sees I'm done with my task, he speeds up his thrusts. I try to hold back my orgasm as the delight builds. The tip of his cock hammers against the magical spot deep inside me, and the pleasure is so intense, I'm going to come at any moment.

A knock at the door shatters my concentration, and I let out an embarrassingly loud groan.

"The clients are here," Mr. Parks calls through the door.

Mr. Jacobs slams into me one last time and groans as he explodes. His warm cum coats my inner walls as he unloads. Ohhhh, no, what? It can't be over.

He jerks against me, unloading ropes of cum before pulling out. I slump down onto the table, squeezing my eyes closed for a moment as I feel his cum leak out of me and drip down my leg. Today really isn't going how I expected. I thought I'd have come at least once by now.

I'm in a daze as I watch him move to a side table and pick up a container of wet wipes I didn't notice before. They aren't usually in here. He was prepared.

As he cleans himself up, he says, casually, "You better make yourself presentable before everyone walk in here."

Fuck, shit. I hastily pull my panties and skirt up, tucking my blouse back in. Mr. Jacobs walks back over to me and whispers in my ear, "I'm not done with you. Go be a good slut and earn your paycheck for the next hour."

He spanks me and I yelp. My legs feel like jelly as I leave. I run into Mr. Parks escorting four other lawyers down the hall. Oh god, is my hair a mess? Heat blooms across my cheeks as I realize my skirt isn't on straight.

Mr. Parks gives me a devilish smile as they pass, and I wish the floor would open up and swallow me, even as a zing of naughty delight turns me on even more. When I reach my desk, I plop down into my seat and feel Mr. Jacobs' cum leaking into my panties. This is messed up in the best of ways.

Instead of tackling my to-do list, I grab my phone from my purse and text my husband.

Miranda:

> I'm sure you'll be happy to know I just got fucked and didn't have time to come.

Jon:

> That's not very nice of them.

The winking emoji he adds tells me he doesn't mean what he's saying.

Miranda:

> I know it's not. Now I have a pussy full of Mr. Jacobs' cum. How am I supposed to work in these conditions?

His reply makes my body buzz with delight.

Jon:

> Send me a picture of that used pussy.

Well, that's hot. I rush to the bathroom and pull my skirt and panties back down before bending over the sink. It takes a couple of tries with the camera behind me, before I get a picture that shows the perfect angle where he can see my swollen, wet pussy.

I send it to him and his reply comes right as I get back to my desk.

Jon:

> Beautiful. I'm heading into a meeting.
> Have fun today, Kitten.

I stare at the wall in a daze. What is my life? I'm a mess. I don't know what's planned and what isn't—is it even a real meeting? It's only 10 a.m. and something tells me it's going to be a long day of sexual torture. I'm 100 percent on board with this plan.

CHAPTER 2

I attempt to work for the next hour, but all I can do is think about being fucked again. Will one of the other lawyers fuck me too, or is today only for Mr. Jacobs? He's no spring chicken, so how many times can he come in a day? He might need a break.

The meeting must be over now, because the hallway fills with sound a moment before the whole group passes my desk on the way out, and I blush, focusing on my computer screen to avoid looking at any of them. Shit, I hope the room didn't smell like sex. I wasn't exactly paying attention when I left.

Once the other lawyers are out of earshot, Mr. Jacobs saunters up to my desk, carrying a bundle of files. "Go clean up the conference room. When you're done, copy all these reports before lunch."

He sets them on my desk and I eye the stack. Oh, I've been here before...I'll clean and then as I'm making copies, someone is going to come in and fuck me against the copier. Just watch.

As he walks off, he adds over his shoulder. "If you get it done by lunch, I'll spank you. If not..."

Well hell, I'm about to be the fastest copy girl ever.

"Yes, sir," I call out sweetly and hurry to clean.

As soon as I step inside the conference room, I'm met with the faint aroma of musk in the air. It smells like me—did all the lawyers notice? I'm suddenly dying of embarrassment. I'm sure they didn't, and I only do because I know what sex with me smells like...right? Right.

The pile of folders I stuffed is at the end of the table and catches my eye. None of them have been touched. Yeah, Mr. Jacobs gave me a stupid task just so he could fuck me. I bet he never planned to let me come.

I'm grumbling to myself as I give the room a cursory cleaning. I can't spend too long in here since I actually want that spanking—and the potential fucking while I make those copies. I grab the files from my desk and dash to the copier machine. I keep one eye on the doorway while I run the files through the machine. Who is going to come in? Maybe Mr. Parks, since he most likely knows what happened in the conference room. I'm on the edge the entire time, just waiting.

No one shows up.

Before I leave the copier room, I check the wall clock. Twenty minutes to spare. Someone could have fucked me, and I still would have gotten done in time. These guys are wasting their opportunities.

I huff and take the copies back to my desk. Before I can sit down, Mr. Jacobs appears. "Bring those with you."

Excitement surges in my veins as I grab the papers and follow him to his office. He steps aside at the doorway and gestures for me to enter his lair. As I pass him, his hand lightly connects with my ass. There'll probably be more of that shortly. I'm not sure I've ever been this eager for a spanking—but then again, have I ever waited two whole years for someone to spank me?

"Put the copies on my desk and then strip." The raw edge in his tone makes me tremble with desire.

Oooh, here we go. He moves behind his desk as I toss the files onto the surface, scattering them haphazardly. I watch with satisfaction as some of the papers slide out.

"Oops, sorry." I try to sound apologetic as I turn around and show him my backside. I'm just ensuring I get a good spanking.

I unzip my skirt ever so slowly and let it fall to the floor as I start to unbutton my shirt. Mr. Jacobs sighs as if I'm exasperating him and says, "Face me."

I spin around and spread my shirt open so he can see my white lace bra. Teasing him is so much fun, and I love riling him up. It will make him all that much rougher when he finally spanks me good.

"Sexy," he says under his breath, his face warming as his eyes feast on my breasts.

That's when it dawns on me. I keep moaning about how Bonny made it so I couldn't fuck my bosses for two years, but it's the same from his side of the fence. It's been a very long time since we've played these games, and he's probably just as wound up as I am. The knowledge sends a ripple of pleasure through me, and I feel like a powerful, sexual goddess.

As soon as I toss my shirt on the floor, he demands, "Come here and put your elbows on my desk."

Oooh, someone is impatient. He didn't even let me undress all the way. I sway my hips as I brush past him and assume the requested position, placing my elbows and palms against the scattered paperwork. I wiggle my backside at him, feeling the stretch of satin and lace across my butt. He caresses my inner thigh before sliding his hand upwards. I rest my forehead on the backs of my hands as a tingling sensation zips straight to my pussy. It's crazy how he only has to touch me and I'm ready to beg him to fuck me.

He hooks a finger into the edge of my panties and pulls it up between the cheeks of my ass. The fabric bunches together and digs into my pussy. Mmm, fuck. I jiggle my ass again, trying to make the fabric rub my clit, but it doesn't move.

He slides a finger into my pussy. "Tell me about Jon."

Jon? Why is he asking about my husband while his finger is inside me?

Before I can ask him why the heck he's bringing this up, he adds another finger. My brain blanks. Uh... what were we talking about? I push my hips back, forcing his fingers in deeper.

He slaps my ass with his free hand, and I wobble in my heels for a moment as heat rushes through me.

"Answer my question."

The spank clears my head and I remember the topic. "Things are going great with Jon."

I'm still not sure why he's asking, and my brain is quickly short-circuiting. Being spanked earlier got me hot and bothered, and I'm still tender from his little show in the conference room.

"How many other guys have you fucked in the last two years?"

I tense, suddenly apprehensive. Where's he going with this?

"Miranda," he growls.

"I don't know," I respond softly. It's weird discussing this with Mr. Jacobs. "The freeuse resort you sent me to had at least a dozen men."

Shit, did all the guys fuck me at the resort? Even though it was only a few weeks ago, my memory of that weekend is a bit hazy. I was so blissed out, I mostly remember the room full of naked guys in Santa hats as they took turns using my mouth.

I rock my hips up and down, trying to force him to finger fuck me harder.

Instead he pulls his hand away. "Naughty slut," he says a moment before his hand connects with my ass.

A pleasurable pain blossoms across my backside and I moan softly. That was a firm hit, and it drives home the fact that he's in charge. My pulse speeds up as I wait to see if he's going to spank me, finger me, or fuck me.

He presses his hand against my pussy, applying pressure but this time he doesn't slide his fingers inside. "You're hoping I fuck you again, aren't you?"

Um... of course I am. I'm not crazy.

I give a breathy, "Please, I want your cock. I'll be a good girl for the rest of the day."

The devil knows that's a promise I'll break at the next available opportunity. But if it gets me fucked or spanked right this moment, I can pretend I'll be good.

He chuckles. "It's a shame you don't deserve it."

I snap my head up and look back at him. Um, what?

My mind spins in confusion as he says, "But I could be convinced and change my mind. Why do you deserve an orgasm?"

He's not supposed to make me justify my desires. He's supposed to just use me! He spanks me again, and I whimper. "I made the folders, set up the coffee, and cleaned."

"Not enough." Another sharp smack.

Shit, what else did I do? I wrack my brain, trying to think of anything else I've done that might warrant a reward. "I...I made copies. I did everything you asked."

"You're missing the point, Miranda."

A painful spank makes me groan as he continues to swat me, alternating cheeks. Each time he makes contact, my ass flares with heat. Within moments, my pussy is practically dripping. I enjoy Mr. Jacobs being grumpy and making me jump through hoops to get what I want... as long as I get what I want eventually.

After a series of powerful strikes, he asks again, "Tell me. What have you done today that deserves an orgasm?"

The correct answer is probably "nothing," since I apparently haven't done enough, but the overwhelming need to be fucked makes me beg. "I'll do anything you want," I babble. "Please..."

Pain explodes across my backside as his hand makes contact again. Ouch. Fuck. Oww. I rest my head on the surface of his desk and close my eyes. Jon never spanks me like this, and something inside me loosens. A warm fuzziness steals over me and I rise above the pain to where all I can feel is pleasure. My awareness narrows to just the satisfying jolts and the slickness between my thighs

I'm shocked when I climax. One second I'm in a peaceful place, and the next moment I'm flying high as an orgasm rockets through me. I cry out as my entire body spasms. Oooh no.

He stops spanking me. "Did you have permission to come?"

I mean, I didn't not have permission. He never said I couldn't. I don't voice my thought. "I'm sorry, sir. I couldn't stop it."

He massages the sore globes of my bottom for a few moments before moving up to unhook my bra. His warm palms caressing my breasts are wonderful, and I relax as he fondles me. At this moment, he really could do whatever he wanted and I'd love it.

CHAPTER 3

I expect Mr. Jacobs to fuck me now that he's spanked me, but he sits in his chair and gives my butt a gentle pat. "Ready to work again?"

Ugh, work. When I try to stand up, he presses his hand on my back. "Stay there. This position is perfect."

A zip of desire runs through me and I relax. I'm up for whatever involves being bent over his desk.

A knock on the door makes me jump, and Mr. Jacobs calls out, "Come in."

Mr. Parks and Mr. Daniels walk in, and take seats across from us. They smile at me as Mr. Jacobs hands me a legal pad and pen. "Take the minutes for our meeting. You'll type them up after."

What kind of meeting are they having with an almost naked woman in front of them? I wiggle my ass to tease Mr. Jacobs. My panties are still wedged together and driving me crazy.

"The clients are demanding..." Mr. Jacobs starts.

Mr. Parks snorts. "They always are."

I'm going to be demanding if I don't get fucked soon. My handwriting is a mess as I try to force myself to follow their boring conversation about a local conference Mr. Daniels is attending tomorrow. When Mr. Jacobs starts fingering my clit, I bite my lip to hold in a moan. I should have expected this.

Mr. Jacobs keeps talking like nothing's happening while he slides his fingers into my pussy and fucks me with them. I struggle to write, my hand shaking from pleasure. It doesn't help that Mr. Daniels and Mr. Parks are watching me. I can tell they're amused.

A jolt of electricity shoots through me as he speeds up his hand movements. My brain goes fuzzy as I barrel towards another orgasm. I can barely manage to write anything. What were they saying?

I'm distracted by the bulges in Mr. Parks' and Mr. Daniels' pants. My mouth waters, imagining sucking them both. Why aren't they all using me if I'm their freeuse toy this week? Or are they taking turns like they used to?

"Miranda." Mr. Jacobs pulls his fingers out and smacks my butt. "Be a good office slut. Crawl over there and take care of them. Your moans are distracting."

Oops, I didn't realize I was moaning. Is he suggesting what I think? I glance over my shoulder at him, questioningly. He gives a slight nod towards the other lawyers. Fuck yes, he wants me to suck their cocks.

I kick off my heels and sink to my knees. Mr. Parks spreads his legs as I crawl over, a thrill shooting through me at the power I wield. My fingers fumble with his belt buckle because I'm so damn eager to get him into my mouth. When I finally free his cock, I pause to appreciate it. He's rock-hard and ready.

I trace my fingertips along his length, savoring the silky texture. God, I love giving blow jobs. A glistening bead forms at the tip, and my mouth waters. I wrap my lips around him, rolling my tongue over the head. He fills my mouth perfectly, and I relish his every twitch and groan. Knowing I'm the source of his pleasure gives me satisfaction. I take him deeper, my own arousal building with each inch.

"Fuck, that's good," he groans, his fingers tangling in my hair.

I hum around him, the vibration making him buck his hips. His reaction spurs me on, and I hollow my cheeks, sucking harder. The taste of him floods my senses, salty and masculine. I press my thighs together, seeking relief. My panties are still bunched up, but they're firmly lodged in a way that only makes me aware of them and doesn't give me enough pleasure.

"Let's finish our meeting," Mr. Jacobs says casually.

They return to their business discussion while I bob my head. I'm getting wetter by the second.

"Miranda, pay attention. You'll still need to write this down," Mr. Jacobs reminds me, with a hint of amusement.

Yeah, these notes I write up later aren't going to be thorough. I'll just have to make them all come so they're happy and don't care. When Mr. Jacobs mentions me going to the conference with Mr. Daniels tomorrow, I perk up. A field trip! Wait... is Mr. Daniels going to fuck me there?

I keep sucking Mr. Parks while daydreaming about being passed around by a dozen horny lawyers. The fantasy makes me quicken my pace, desperate to taste his cum.

"Fuck, I'm close," Mr. Parks hisses.

I double my efforts, my hand working what my mouth can't reach. His hips flex, and I know he's right there. With a final groan, he explodes, flooding my mouth. I swallow greedily, not wanting to waste a drop.

As his grip on my hair loosens, I give him one last lick and pull back with a smile. "Mmm...tasty."

I'm dying for a cock to fuck me—anyone's cock—but Mr. Daniels is staring at me hungrily. Without being told, I crawl between his legs.

Mr. Jacobs sighs. "Suck him off. Make it quick."

That's not quite what I had in mind, but oh well. Mr. Daniels pulls out his thick cock for me, and I eagerly take him into my mouth, savoring his salty taste and the difference between the two men's cocks. He moans when I take him deep, his tip hitting the back of my throat. I cup his balls as I bob faster, determined to make him come quickly. It doesn't take long before his thigh muscles tense and he blows his load. I clean him up with my tongue before sitting back. That was a job well done, if I do say so myself.

The men look well satisfied—well, not Mr. Jacobs. And where is Mr. King today? Why wasn't he at the meeting? I wait for instructions as Mr. Daniels and Mr. Parks straighten their clothes and leave. I guess the meeting is over.

"Think you can write a coherent report?" Mr. Jacobs asks.

I stay silent. Uhh, doubtful. But I can wing it. He beckons me over and I crawl to him, hoping he'll let me suck his dick next. To my surprise, he pulls out a packet of trail mix from his desk drawer and feeds it to me while I kneel on the floor next to him.

Between bites, I ask, "What's this about the conference, sir?"

My pussy throbs, craving his cock. I need to come so badly. Hopefully once he stops feeding me, he'll fuck me.

"We thought our freeuse toy might like an outing," he says. "Have some fun outside the office."

Uh... "Fun with other lawyers?" If this is some gangbang, I need to talk to Jon.

Mr. Jacobs laughs. "No, just Mr. Daniels. You'll have to be discreet. Think you can manage that?"

"I'll be the most discreet slut ever," I promise.

"We're counting on it." He touches my cheek gently, making my stomach flutter. Then his voice turns stern. "Now go type those notes. Email them to me and be back here in fifteen minutes."

"Yes, sir." The air crackles between us—we both know what's coming when I return.

"Leave your clothes. You'll get them when the report's done."

Oooh, fuck. My heart races as I murmur, "Yes, sir."

He nods, satisfied. "Good. Now get to work."

I walk to my desk, hyperaware I'm only wearing my panties. What if a client shows up? My nipples harden from the thrill of possible exposure. My pussy is drenched and I eye my office chair. Do men even think of these problems? Just go type these up, he says... how am I supposed to sit on my chair like this?

Fuck. I sneak to the break room and grab a cardigan I brought in last week and forgot on the coat rack, tying it around my waist as a makeshift skirt. Not perfect, but it'll do. I rush back, my heart pounding with nervous excitement. The risk of getting caught sends shivers down my spine.

I sit down, glad for the extra padding against my sore ass, and start typing. I try to remember the meeting details through my sex-fogged brain, but the taste of cum in my mouth and the wetness between my legs cloud my thoughts.

I'm almost done when footsteps approach. Shit. Shit. Shit. My heart leaps as Mr. King walks up.

"Miranda, are the notes ready? Mr. Jacobs told me to ask you for a copy," he says casually, though his gaze lingers on my body.

I swallow hard. "Almost. I can email them to you shortly."

He nods, his eyes dropping to my breasts. "You're making me wish it was my turn with you again."

Ooh, so they ARE taking turns. My body vibrates with delight at the thought.

Once he leaves, I quickly finish and email Mr. Jacobs and Mr. King. I'm sure it's missing details, but it's the best I could do under the circumstances. I rush back to Mr. Jacobs' office, leaving the cardigan behind. That thing needs a good wash now.

I knock softly before entering. He looks up, his expression hardened. "Those notes were unacceptable. You missed half the conversation."

No shit. I clasp my hands, purposely making my breasts squish together. "I'm sorry, sir. I was distracted."

By his fingers in my pussy before I sucked on two cocks.

"Come here."

His expression is unreadable and he stands as I come around to his side. He slides my panties down my legs and I step out of them. When he lifts me onto his desk, I wince as the hard wood presses against my tender backside.

He grins and spreads my knees. Yeah, he knows my ass hurts. He kisses my neck. "Did you think if you looked sexy that I wouldn't notice how bad of a job you did?"

I shiver, my body responding to him. "I'm sorry, sir. I can try again—"

"Try again?" His look turns predatory. "Or maybe I'll just fuck you to remind you who's in charge."

Yep, I like his plan better. He pushes me back onto the desk so that I'm lying down and tugs me to the edge. His fingers probe my pussy, making him growl, "You're so fucking wet."

I squirm, aching for more. "Please fuck me, sir."

He pulls out his cock, stroking it slowly. "You need this?"

"Yes, please." I nod eagerly and wrap my legs around him.

He taps the head against my clit. "Beg for it."

I gyrate my hips and whimper, "Please, sir. Please fuck me. I need your cock inside me. I'll do better next time. Please just fuck me."

He grasps my waist with both hands and thrusts in hard. "Ooooh, god," I cry out and arch my back as he starts fucking me fast and rough. I throw my hands over my head so I can hold on to the desk's edge as he ravages me. The sound of skin slapping fills the room as I get closer to my climax.

"You're such a good little slut. You love being fucked like this, don't you?"

I gasp, "Yes, so good," as the pressure builds with each stroke. I'm ready to explode.

He reaches between my legs to rub my clit. "Show me how much you love being our office slut and come for me."

The combined stimulation is too much. Ecstasy rips through me, and I come so hard I see stars. I convulse around his cock as he fucks me through my orgasm.

He doesn't slow down. "You're going to come once more before I fill you up and send you home to your husband."

The desk creaks as he hammers into me and continues to rub my clit. Another orgasm builds as I think about going home to Jon full of Mr. Jacobs' cum. My husband is going to love hearing about my day.

Mr. Jacobs is relentless, and time loses meaning. I play with my nipples, and chant, "Oh my god," as delight twists in my core. He's hitting the good spot deep inside me repeatedly, and I'm ready to come.

His thrusts become shorter, and I finally snap. I scream as another orgasm tears through me. He pulls out slowly without coming, and I feel a rush of wetness leaking out. I hope he has some of those wet wipes in here.

"Look at you, all fucked and messy," he says, appreciatively. "You want more, don't you? You want me to fuck you like the slut you are?"

"Yes, please."

He grabs my arms and pulls me up from the desk. His eyes are heavy with lust, mirroring the hunger in my own. He lifts me off my feet, and I hook my legs around his waist, crossing my ankles behind his back.

His hands grip my butt, fingers digging into the tender flesh as he holds me up. I can feel his hard cock pressing against my entrance, and I'm desperate for him to fill me again.

"Where should I fuck you next?"

He sounds like he's talking to himself, but I answer anyway. "Everywhere."

He carries me over to the couch that was recently added to his office, laying me down on my back. He slowly takes his clothes off and I watch him, curious to see if he looks different than I remember. He's still fit and trim, and I can tell he still exercises regularly.

Once he's naked, he looks down at me and commands, "Spread your legs for me."

I obey, letting him see how swollen and wet my pussy is. He kneels between my legs and moves his face to my pussy. I can feel his breath on my sensitive flesh, and I shiver with anticipation.

"You're absolutely gorgeous like this," he groans. He leans in and licks a slow path up my pussy, my hips rocking as he teases me.

"God, you're delicious." He dips his tongue inside me, and I reach down to grip his hair as he feasts on me.

He pulls back, holding my gaze. "You want my cock, don't you? You want me to fuck you until you can't think straight?"

I'm so turned on, all I can do is say, "Yes."

In reality, he can do whatever he wants. I'm beyond caring. He could stop right now, and I'd probably just thank him for using me.

He grabs my legs, pushing my knees towards my chest and I can feel myself opening up for him.

He slams into me, his hips pistoning as he fucks me hard and fast. I can feel every inch of him, every ridge and vein as he slides in and out of me.

He leans forward, holding onto my thighs as he uses them for leverage. His thrusts become harder and I continuously moan in pleasure.

"You feel so good." His muscles strain as he pounds into me.

I take back everything I thought earlier about him being the oldest. This guy is a machine. He has me pinned to the couch and at his mercy. It's amazing.

"You're just our little toy, a plaything to use whenever we need a release," he groans, and my body lights up at his words.

I gasp when he hits a pleasurable spot repeatedly, and my head spins. He teased me for hours, but this was worth the wait.

"You like that, don't you?" he asks. "Knowing we're going to use you all the time." The raw need in his husky voice sends another tremor of pleasure along my spine.

"Yes, I'm your fucktoy to use. Want it!"

I'd say anything, do anything, I just need to come again, and I need him to fill me up. I can tell the next orgasm is going to be massive. My body is on fire, every nerve ending alive as the tension coils tighter and tighter.

I'm ready to fall, and I moan, "Feels so good."

His tone is harsh as he hammers into me. "Come for me, you little slut. Come for me NOW."

"Fuck!" I scream, as my body shudders. The pleasure is so intense I see flashes of light behind my eyelids as I ride the waves of rapture. It might have lasted a few seconds, or a minute, I'm so far gone it feels like it's never ending.

With a final, deep thrust, he finds his own release. It seems like he's fucking me forever, unloading ropes and ropes of cum inside me, filling me up.

I'm shivering when he collapses on top of me. We're a tangle of limbs and sweat, our breathing ragged and uneven. I can feel him still inside me, his cock slowly softening as we both come down from the high.

I'm not sure how long we lie there, blissed out. But eventually his lips brush against my ear.

"You're amazing," he whispers.

A warmth spreads through me as he helps me sit up. When he kisses me, I'm not expecting it. It's a gentle kiss, but thorough, and as our tongues twirl together, I realize this is something I'm going to have to tell Jon about. Mr. Jacobs has changed over the last two years. There's an unexpected softness to him, but I think I'm going to enjoy it. He can still spank me and fuck me hard, and I know Jon is fine with my play partners being tender towards me.

Mr. Jacobs breaks off the kiss, and murmurs, "Good girl. Now I'm sending you home early because you need a good night's sleep for the conference tomorrow."

Ooh, yeah, the conference. I'm still tingling from my orgasms and give him a saucy smile. "Yes, sir. Thank you, sir."

He laughs and helps me stand up. "Now clean up and go home."

When he hands me my clothes, my body aches pleasantly as I slowly dress. As I leave his office, I make sure to sway my hips so he gets a nice view...and I want him thinking about spanking me again sometime soon.

CHAPTER 4

I call Jon on my drive home, putting him on speaker.

"Hey, Kitten. How was your day?"

The sound of his voice instantly turns me on again, and my body hums with lust. "Eventful. I've got stories to tell."

He laughs. "I'm sure you do, and I can't wait to hear them. Bad news though, I'm stuck here. I might be late."

My excitement deflates. "Nooo, you need to be home soon."

"I know, I'm sorry. I'll make it up to you later, promise."

I sigh and grumble, "Fine. Guess I'll have to entertain myself. Blame work if I'm too exhausted when you get home."

He teases, "Start without me, but you aren't allowed to finish until I get there."

Shit. Heat pools between my thighs. "Hurry home."

"Will do, Kitten. Love you."

"Love you too," I say, hanging up as I pull into our driveway.

As soon as I'm inside the house, I head for the bedroom, removing my clothes as I go. I don't bother putting anything on. I lie back on the bed, letting my mind wander over the day's events—the spankings, the thrill of fucking Mr. Jacobs again. I slide my hand down to my clit, teasing myself, but it's not enough. I grab my phone and text Jon.

Miranda:

You leaving yet?

He responds instantly.

Jon:

Yes, fuck work. I'm walking out the door right now. Keep that pussy warm for me.

Oooh, nice. His office is only 15 minutes away. I play with myself, moving my hand slowly so I don't accidentally come.

I hear the garage door open and then Jon is in the room, looking as eager as I feel.

"Hey, Kitten," he says in that husky tone of his that tells me he's half crazed already.

I spread my legs wider and he eyes my pussy as he strips. I bet he's trying to see some of my boss's cum.

Once he's naked, he crawls onto the bed next to me and kisses me deeply. I taste his urgency, his need. I love how much he gets turned on by me fucking other people.

Between kisses, he growls, "Tell me everything."

He slips his hand between my legs, and I arch against him as he rubs my clit. How am I supposed to think, let alone talk, while he's touching me? But this is the game we play, and I'm going to tell him everything because that's what keeps our relationship strong.

As he trails kisses down my neck, across my collarbone, and to my breast, I tell him about my day. "I was bent over the desk, and they had a meeting while Mr. Jacobs fingered me."

"Mmm, nice," he moans and takes a nipple into his mouth. He sucks hard and pleasure shoots straight to my core.

While I tell him about the conference and sucking on the lawyers during the meeting, he continues to tease me, circling my clit, dipping his fingers inside me and making me squirm.

I rock against him. "Jon...please."

His eyes smolder with need. "Please what, Kitten?"

"Fuck me," I beg. "Need you inside me."

He grins and positions himself, fitting his cock against my pussy. He doesn't make me wait, and he presses in slowly—oh god, I wish he would pound into me. I love it when he fucks me slow, and yet I also hate it.

As he thrusts into me at his own pace, his cock hits all the right places. I wrap my legs around him and hold onto his shoulders, pulling him closer. Our moans fill the room. I'm close, so close.

I whimper, "Oh, god. I'm almost there."

He looks at me with a fierce expression. "Thank me for letting you fuck your bosses."

"Thank you," I gasp out, my body trembling with the effort to hold back my orgasm. "Thank you for letting me be their fucktoy."

He speeds up slightly, his thrusts hitting me deeper. "That's right, Kitten. You're my little slut, and I love sharing you."

His words send me spiraling and I mewl out in pleasure.

"Good girl," he murmurs. "Now come for me."

I cry out and let go, writhing as the pleasure explodes through me.

My orgasm triggers his. "Fuck, Miranda," he gasps, his cock pulsing inside me, filling me with cum.

We rock together as he finishes unloading, and when he rolls off me, he pulls me close. I'm a puddle of joy as I lay my head on his chest, listening to his heartbeat slow.

"So, tell me more about tomorrow," he says, his voice rumbling under my ear.

I smile, tracing hearts on his chest. "I'll be going with Mr. Daniels. Mr. Jacobs said we'll need to be discreet."

"I'm sure you can handle that," he chuckles. "I want you to have fun, so be their good little slut."

"I will," I purr, snuggling closer.

He kisses the top of my head. "And call me when you get home tomorrow. I want to hear all about it."

"Always, my love."

As we lie there, basking in the afterglow, a sense of contentment washes over me. This is what I love about our relationship. The openness, the trust, the shared pleasure. I'm truly living my best life as a hotwife. And I'm looking forward to whatever happens at the conference. I'm ready to be a slut again for Mr. Daniels.

The End

About Lacey Cross

Lacey Cross is a wife-sharing erotica writer with over 100 short stories published since she started in 2021. Her stories emphasize the pleasure found from the wife living her best slut life and embracing the hotwife lifestyle. She explores themes of free use, submissive wives with dominant bulls, BDSM... and oh-so-many men.

Find her books, erotic shorts, and audiobooks on her website: https://lacey-cross.com/

If you like romantic BDSM erotica, check out her April Cross books at:

https://april-cross.com/